The Adventures of the Nutters

The
Tree Highway

Patrick Ringley & Anne Corbett Brown
Illustrated by Sue Lynn Cotton

enjoy!
Sue Cotton

the Peppertree Press
Sarasota, Florida

1

www.paracba.com

For information regarding permission,
call 941-922-2662 or contact us at our website:
www.peppertreepublishing.com or write to:
the Peppertree Press, LLC.
Attention: Publisher
1269 First Street, Suite 7
Sarasota, Florida 34236

ISBN: 978-1-61493-207-9

Library of Congress Number: 2013915030

Printed in the U.S.A.

Printed September 2013

this story is dedicated to the
hope of finding the "child" in all!

signed,
anne, pat, and "the nutters"

CHAPTER 1

AND SO, THE JOURNEY BEGINS

Once upon a time in a land far away…Wait a minute, this isn't about a land far away!

This is about last week, in a neighborhood, just down the street.

This is about that vacant wooded lot on a busy street.

This is about a family who has to move to have the life they know. Fright builds as the dad, mom, brother, and sister must find a new home. For generations they have laughed, run, and played on their wooded lot, and it has been their beloved home.

Where will they go? How will they get there?

You see, this is about the family of the Nutters—they are squirrels.

The dad needs advice and help to get his family to the new safe woods.

The mom must find a way to help and keep their children safe.

The kids, Rockit and Roxie, just want to play.

All they know is playing and the safety of Mom and Dad keeping their young lives safe.

They don't know how to get to the fabled safe forest.

Granddad Squirrel always said there is a way to the safe woods without coming down to the ground.

Is this possible?

Some say yes.

Some say no.

No one knows for sure, as the city coming closer has changed many things.

Could the fabled way to the safe woods still exist?

There's no choice but to start out.

Dad, Mom, Rockit, and Roxie must gather up as many nuts and berries they can and start out.

"Will we be OK, Dad? Will we be safe, Mom?"

"Where will we sleep?"

"I'm scared," they cried.

Dad and Mom did the best they could to make them comfortable, but the truth was, they were nervous too!

This is the adventure of the Nutters as they set out on the "Tree

HOME
SWEET
HOME

Highway," a legendary path amongst the tops of the tallest pines, the largest oaks, up where the birds live.

Coming down to the ground was dangerous, as it was surrounded with dogs, cats, and many dangers. There was no choice but to leave immediately, as the sound of chain saws, trucks, and bulldozers was coming.

The Tree Highway was all there was to get them to the safe woods.

And so their journey begins.

CHAPTER 2

THE ADVENTURE

The rustling, tossing, and turning crowded the night as Rockit and Roxie knew this was the last night in the tree they called home.

It wasn't much, but it was the only home they knew.

All to be abandoned, all the memories of hide and seek.

All the chasing each other up and down the limbs.

All the swinging from limb-to-limb.

All to be gone until replaced in the fabled woods at the end of the Tree Highway.

They looked at the walls inside the top of the old withered oak they lived.

Many times it sheltered them as they snuggled on the cold winter nights, the rainy days, and it was their hiding place from the hungry hawks and owls.

As it was certain they were leaving, where would they be tomorrow night?

They had to, as their home had the dreadful yellow marker to be cut first.

Dad and Mom prepared but couldn't sleep either.

It was the last time they would call the old gray oak home.

The night passed slowly. They needed more rest than anyone could get.

The one thing they did have was some experience to jump from limb-to-limb, grasping vines, and getting far down the path to security on the Tree Highway.

As the dark became light, they could hear the owls and hawks.

All the birds of prey knew all the squirrels had to leave and it was scary for all.

As Rockit, Roxie, Dad, and Mom thought of travel, the hawks and owls thought of breakfast.

CHAPTER 3

WHO'S THAT?

Tap! Tap! Tap!

"Dad! Someone's at the door."

"Who are you?"

"I'm Annie."

The entire Nutter family was astounded.

A young woodpecker was at the door.

"May I come in?"

"Well, OK."

"Let me explain," said young Annie, "A year ago I was looking for my mom to come and bring me my supper. Out of nowhere, a big hawk grabbed me. My dad saw this and collided with the hawk to rescue me and I fell to the ground, as I could not fly. No one saw where I fell.

But to my surprise, the lady in the house saw all of it. She came out and she and her husband rescued me. I was scared to death—a hawk tries to eat me, then HUMANS!!!!"

"To my surprise, they protected me, made me a bed, fed me, and took me to a shelter, but I lost my mom and dad. Upon returning me to my tree, it was decided the tree was unsafe, so back to the shelter I went. They released me days later when I could fly."

"I returned to my tree and it had fallen."

"I had no idea how to find my family."

"Now I have heard all are leaving here to go to new homes."

"I also heard the Nutters have the secret way to the fabled woods!"

"They have a way to know the Tree Highway, safe from most predators but not all."

"I have known for months my mom and dad are there, but I do not know the way."

"May I come along with you squirrels?"

"I can fly ahead like the best Indian scout and come back and help you."

"I can fly down and get berries to bring!"

"You little ones, yes, you two, Rockit and Roxie, you need your fruit, for squirrels cannot live on nuts and acorns alone!"

Upon hearing young Annie's plight, a resounding "Yes" was heard.

For Rockit and Roxie, it was a new friend with new adventures to share and show.

For Dad, it was a blessing of information of what could be ahead.

For Mom, it was additional help with food for the family.

And so was born the unusual pairing of a young woodpecker, two squirrels, Rockit and Roxie, and a mom and dad.

They all comforted each other as the journey was about to begin.

They all prayed for each other's safety and that young Annie would find her family in the fabled woods!

Annie heard it was a thing called a conservation area, safe for all creatures of the earth never to be torn apart.

In a few minutes, the unlikely troupe was to start out.

Limb-by-limb, jump, run, swing, and travel east towards the sunrise, where the promised forest was said to be.

"Well," Dad said, "as journeys start with the first step, let's go!"

Annie was beyond happy and grateful—it wasn't her family, but as close is it can get.

She felt an instant love for the Nutters. She wasn't a squirrel, their color or type, but love is deeper than any of those things. Love is the spirit of respect and seeking of common family. In this case, it was a magic undefined.

They all looked east at the morning sunrise and away they went.

CHAPTER 4

BEAUTIFUL MORNING

What a morning!

The sun was shining through the hundreds of limbs.

It was the brightest of aqua blues.

The dew was like diamonds and it was time to go.

The Nutters and the lonely little woodpecker were off on the journey of their lives, destination—the fabled safe woods.

The old gray oak was very tall.

They lived almost at the top.

9

Dad took the lead and started jumping from limb-to-limb, headed east. Rockit and Roxie were next with Mom taking the rear and Annie? She flew high above the trees searching for all things good, bad, and worthy of notice.

It was many miles to the fabled woods and would take several days to get there.

They would have to come to the ground sometime and Annie was the safeguard of when, where, and if it was as safe as it could be.

There would be dogs, cats, owls, and hawks.

The dogs were easy, as they could be outrun.

The cats were more troublesome, as they were extremely clever as hunters and they can climb.

The owls and hawks were the worst.

It was just such a hawk, who had separated Annie from her family.

Rockit and Roxie loved little Annie. She could fly.

They were so envious as they jumped from limb-to-limb.

They could catch the smallest of limbs and catapult to the next limb, but Annie could fly.

She could have left the little squirrels to themselves and wandered in the sky until she found the fabled woods. Instead, she chose to be part of the family and stay close, as they all wanted a new home.

"Annie! You can fly!" Rockit was so impressed.

"Rockit!" responded Annie, "you can eat with your paws! I have to do everything with my beak."

"You have teeth! I have to swallow everything almost whole."

They both laughed as Dad said, "Yeah, yeah, yeah."

"The grass is greener on the other side."

The one thing they all knew was the grass would be greener in the fabled woods.

So they pushed forward, limb-by-limb, while Annie flew far ahead.

They thought they had lost her. When she returned, she was so excited, because she found a hedge of wild berries. It would be lunch for all, but it was on the ground and many other birds, raccoons, and all the residents of the woods might be there.

It could be dangerous, so extreme care and lookout was necessary.

CHAPTER 5

RED RASPBERRIES

Midday and so far nothing but progress. Rockit and Roxie were having so much fun, they almost forgot they had no place to sleep tonight.

Annie was the joy for them as she soared high above the tallest trees. Dad was cheerfully leading all, and Mom? She knew it was time for all to eat.

And there it was!

Thirty feet below the limbs they were on, they could see it!

"RED RASPBERRIES!" screamed Rockit.

They were a rare find and like candy to the little squirrels.

They must go to the ground, always a danger, but Annie was to stay circling above and warn of any danger.

Down they went. The berries were still plentiful, but it was easy to see they were popular with all the woods creatures.

Rockit couldn't eat fast enough, "YUM!!" He was in heaven.

Roxie was stuffing them in so fast, she turned her whole face raspberry red.

Dad was on alert, but still ate.

Mom was just plain happy to see the little ones fed.

Annie would swoop down, grab a few, then perch atop a tree, tip her head back and swallow.

All was well for the little family and their adopted member, Annie.

Dad said, "Let's go, we must leave some for the other travelers."

The trees were becoming full of all who left the old woods.

Annie and the Nutters decided to rest atop an old pine tree and an older woodpecker arrived.

Annie was thrilled, she loved seeing anyone like her.

She was excited to introduce her new family.

The older woodpecker asked where Annie's family was.

She said she was kidnapped by a hawk before she could fly.

Her dad attacked the big hawk, the hawk dropped her 25 feet to the ground, and took off after her dad.

"I never knew if my dad got away or if he's still alive."

"I was saved by a nice lady who fed me and made sure I was safe. When I was returned and able to fly, my old home was unsafe. It soon

fell to the ground and lays there still today. Without the nice lady, I would have been eaten by the hawk, but I was rescued so fast that when the hawk returned, I was already in the lady's house."

"Humans have a thing call furniture, and things that may light in the dark. She went to this big box that was full of food and fed me some things and gave me some milk. I was scared, but somehow they made me feel OK. The nice lady called a bird rescue to give me shelter until I could fly. The lady was sad to see me go, but knew it was the right thing to do. When the animal shelter brought me back, I was amazed how happy the nice lady was to see me."

"I could never find my mom, didn't know if the hawk killed my dad, and flew alone, looking with the hope of a miracle that somehow I would find my family."

"Then, when I heard the old woods was to be torn down, I returned with one last hope I could find any of my family."

"While watching Rockit and Roxie play, I felt an instant connection."

"Their joy, so large for life, their love of their mom and dad, made me realize they weren't woodpeckers, but they were wonderful loving creatures of the woods."

"So I introduced myself and they adopted me as though I was one of them."

"Well, my little young friend, I know this story. In the fabled woods, there is a family who lost their daughter in just such a way."

"REALLY!" said Annie.

"YES!" said the old woodpecker.

"They live in the bright corner that sees the sunrise first every day."

"I know them—they hope, dream, and pray that someday they will find their daughter."

"How do I know they are your parents?"

"How many woodpeckers could have a daughter named Annie that was caught in such a tale!"

"ROCKIT, ROXIE!! DAD!!! MOM!!! Did you hear this!! My parents are alive and well in the fabled woods!"

Dad knew that with so much in their bellies, so much good news, and yet still so much uncertainty, they should rest for the night.

Annie flew ahead and found an old abandoned treetop.

The old tree was hit by lightning and was hollow at the top.

No one could see it and it was as good as one could hope.

They all snuggled together, Annie was right there by their side.

How could she sleep? The news of her parents' safety filled her heart and soul with a joy undefined.

She could have flown ahead, but would not leave the Nutters behind.

She had pledged her help to scout safe passage and would never break her word.

So as the full moon rose, the family fell asleep.

As Mom looked at the walls, she was teary, as she missed the old oak tree where she raised Rockit and Roxie. Dad knew she was sad to leave the home of her memories and comforted her.

"Mom, you must always remember, home is with your family, love is with them and no object."

"We can find another home, but not another Rockit and Roxie."

Annie knew this so well and now she was on the path to find her family.

CHAPTER 6

REBEL

"Roxie!! Wake up, you got to see this!"

"What, Rockit?"

"It looks like heaven!"

The morning clouds high in the sky were the brightest day-glow orange with aquamarine blue the little squirrels had ever seen.

Rockit was convinced it was a sign leading to the fabled woods.

"What's all the excitement about?" asked Dad.

"The sky, Dad!! The sky," said Rockit, "It's a map to our new home."

"Could be you two… could be…"

"We must get up and get going."

Then, flying back in for a third time, was newly adopted Nutter, Annie.

She was an early bird, as the saying goes, but was not bringing worms.

She had flown back to the berries and brought breakfast for all.

Annie was truly sent from the heavens to help the squirrel family, and help she was doing.

As they were all eating, they heard someone coming up the old hollow tree.

As it got closer, there was a very angry, "HEY, what are you doing in my pad?"

As they looked, they could see a very sarcastic angry little face.

"Who do you squirrels think you are, crashing into my place?"

"Well," said dad, "no one was here, so we thought…"

"Yeah, you thought!"

Dad replied, "Well, where were you all night?"

The little angry squirrel said, "Like that's any of your business, Captain."

Now Dad was getting angry, this was no way to start the day.

Roxie then said, "Hey, you can't talk to my dad like that."

"Easy, Buttercup."

"I'm Rebel, the coolest swinging squirrel in the woods."

Dad is now extremely angry.

"You can't talk to my daughter like that!"

As usual, Mom intervenes.

"Well, Rebel, would you like to join us for breakfast?"

"You bet, sweetie!"

Dad is angry, "Hey, Rebel, we are trying to get to the fabled woods. We are using the Tree Highway, and you are making the day a bummer with all your bad manners."

Hey, Captain, why the Tree Highway?"

Dad responded, "So the little ones don't have to go to the ground where it's dangerous."

"WRONG, Captain, that changed some time back by the same humans that most likely cut your tree down."

"You will have to go to the ground two times, once on a small road and then at a busy road where there are some businesses."

"How do you know this, Rebel?"

I go to the fabled woods all the time. There's some foxy gals there."

"It is two days as the crow flies, but you jerks are squirrels, so who knows how long it will take this little circus act."

"This is a horrible start to the day!" said Mom.

"Dad, you quiet down! Rebel, would you like to join us and help show us the way?"

"Well, Sweetie, with a face like yours and a foxy gal like Roxie, I'm in."

Dad quietly hated this, but was realizing as he was raised to be kind to all, he must accept Rebel.

Maybe Rebel never had a dad or a mom or any family and was a smart aleck as part of his only way to survive.

So off they went, Dad, Mom, Roxie, Rockit, Annie flying point, and now Rebel, a punk squirrel.

It was an east start as the tall pines touched and jumping from limb to limb was not only easy, but fun.

And, as expected, Rebel was showing off.

He would do triple summersaults, hang upside down, fall almost to the ground and run back up the next limb.

Rockit wanted to try this, Roxie was impressed, and Annie could easily see Roxie was getting smitten by the bad boy.

The day went along without incident and progress being made, the first road was coming up.

Rebel stopped the group to tell them the trees were cut back and it was only the ground to get across. This frightened Roxie.

Rebel said, "Hey, sweet cheeks, I'll make sure you are safe."

Dad felt Rebel was invading his duty.

Mom was happy for his offer of help.

Rockit didn't know what to think. He just thought in all of the faults, Rebel was kind of cool.

Annie stayed out—she just kept flying, looking for any dangers.

She had already swooped down at a few cats that were stalking the family and they didn't know it.

CHAPTER 7

THE ESCAPE

Well, it was time to do it.

"RUN!" screamed Dad.

Out of the hollow treetop they went, scrambling in every direction, but aiming forward.

Boris, angry, wet, and tired from perching all night, launched downward as the troupe hit the ground. He swooped down in a starved anger and as all thought, Roxie was the target.

She was frightened to no end and ran faster than she ever had, faking left, then right, but to no avail, as the long razor-sharp claws caught her.

Rebel was furious. He charged to bump Roxie from the grip of Boris.

He jumped and missed. A sadness drowned all, as fear took over.

Then, out of nowhere it seemed, little Annie swooped and body-slammed Boris.

He lost his grip and little Roxie fell many feet to the ground. Stunned and frightened, she just laid there. Boris was beyond angry as he darted back.

Then a real surprise! One of Boris' main rivals, the old grumpy lady owl, Martha, even larger than Boris, hit him midflight, so hard he crashed to the forest floor.

Now we have pandemonium.

Rebel got Roxie up. Dad, Mom, and Rockit have everyone revived.

Rebel says, "Follow me now!"

He seemed to know more than any about every detail of not only the Tree Highway, but the thick forest floor.

They all ran darting again, left then right.

Sure enough, Rebel led them to an old hollow tree that was on the ground.

The entry was small, so the birds couldn't get in.

In there they caught their breath.

"Wait!" said Dad, "What's that?"

They all looked into the other end of the log and saw two scary eyes.

It was a possum, but it was no real threat. After what they just went through, they didn't want anything scary.

"I'm Wilbur, I say, Wilbur Possum. I heard what just happened. I mean you no harm and besides, I'm half-blind."

"Boris scratched my eyes and I can barely see, so I just stay in here and only go out when I must find food." Wilbur pretty much lived on bugs.

Well, as Annie heard this, she flew out amidst all danger and came back with some bugs for Wilbur. He was so happy, as he had no friends.

The Nutters, Rebel, and Annie, said, "Well, you do today."

"We are taking the Tree Highway to the fabled woods."

Wilbur was sad, as he couldn't go, but he couldn't climb trees or see well enough.

Annie promised to come back and visit from time to time to make sure Wilbur was never too lonely.

"Then," Rebel said, "we still have those two out there. We must get past them in a distance where they won't know where we are."

And then out of nowhere comes a black-and-white spotted dog, Sak. Now Sak lived to chase squirrels for fun. She was gentle and wouldn't hurt a flea. She also, though fast, was no match for any squirrel. Rebel was sure if they got Sak running, the birds would not come close.

It was a gamble, but it was all they had.

"All right, is everyone ready?" Rebel and Dad went first.

Then Mom, Rockit, and Roxie, then Annie flying fast to create a diversion.

"Good luck," said Wilbur.

Sure enough, when Sak saw them, she ran skipping and jumping and barking. Every squirrel made it to the next stand of tall trees and they gathered at the top. Sak stood there looking up, barking. This was enough to get Boris and Martha to drop their pursuit.

They knew as tough as they were, one good bite from a dog could be too much for them.

As the troupe sat resting, Rebel wanted to know where and how Annie knew of such a body slam that saved Roxie.

"Well," said Rebel, "I saw my dad do it to a large hawk who grasped me from my home as I was waiting for my mom to feed me, and I never saw my mom and dad again."

"Now it's possible they live in the fabled woods and nothing will stop me from finding out!"

It was close to night as they journeyed on.

Rebel once again found a suitable place to stay.

They all snuggled together as one big family, Annie nesting beside them.

"Tomorrow we come to our first road to cross."

"The trees have been cut back so it's down to the ground and across the road with cars, our worst problem," said Rebel.

"But don't worry, I do it all the time."

"Do what I do and it will be OK."

With that, they all dozed off, wondering when they would get to the fabled woods.

"Two days," said Rebel, "two days and one more road."

CHAPTER 8

DANGER

As the sun peaked over the eastern sky, all awoke. The day before escaping Boris, Martha, and facing tragedy was in all of their thoughts, as the journey must continue to the fabled woods.

It was misty and a bit chilly.

There were some leaves to munch on and some broad leaves holding dew from the night.

Rebel was anxious to go and felt a new life, as the Nutters were greatly helped by his knowledge of the path.

The trees were now very tall and close together. Jumping from limb-to-limb was easy, so off they went.

"We will get to the small but traveled road by midday," said Rebel.

"It's important you listen and follow my advice."

Dad and Mom had crossed roads, but not very much.

The old gray oak was off the road that was in front, so there was no reason to cross.

Food was plentiful, so they stayed safely around the tree.

Rockit and Roxie had never tried to get across dealing with cars.

Annie stayed high above, dreaming of the day she might be reunited with her parents.

Lilting and swaying from branch-to-branch was so enjoyable that they all forgot the day before and running for their lives.

There was no sign of Boris or Martha and the speed of the squirrels was hopefully good enough to avoid attack.

Then it could be heard—trucks and cars rolling down a small road.

It was approaching lunchtime, so traffic was up as the humans were going to the stores in a distant town.

It was now down to the ground and sizing up the crossing.

It was about the height of a tree to the pavement, then hot asphalt as the day warmed up, then another run to the next part of the Tree Highway.

The trees were close but lined large fields of perfect short grass.

There were people playing a game called golf.

This was good as they kept many hunting animals away.

On part of the Tree Highway, there were large homes for the humans. It was a country club neighborhood.

Dad, Mom, Rockit, and Roxie had never seen one of these.

"Oh, they are quite normal in this part of the Tree Highway."

"But they do have human children who find it fun to shoot BB guns at us and throw rocks."

"We are nothing but some game of target practice, so we must look out for this."

"One good thing is we are small squirrels. Way up north some of our relatives are five times our size and humans hunt them for food."

Rockit and Roxie were terrified to hear any of this. Annie was in a better frame of mind.

She said, "Well, I'm on the endangered species list and humans are in BIG trouble if they even think of hurting a woodpecker."

The problem she had thought was, this didn't apply to hawks and, thusly, she was orphaned but just such a situation.

It was time to cross.

"OK" said Rebel, "We are going to cross one at a time."

"Do what I do, and watch carefully."

"Do not get to the middle, get frightened, and stop or go back."

"You must look out for the car and run between it and the next one."

Well, this was NOT going to work for Roxie.

"Dad, can you please stay next to me?"

"OK, Roxie."

Rebel decided he would stay on her other side. So that was the decision.

A large pickup truck was coming. The next car was not that far behind, but they decided to go for it anyway.

Off they went as fast as their little paws could move.

Roxie panicked, the truck was huge, shaking the ground. As she looked up at the back of it, she froze and wanted to go back.

"NO, Roxie, you have to move and move now!"

The next car sped over all of them. One of the tires nicked Rebel's tail.

23

"OUCH!!!!!!!!" He was OK, but being street smart, he had nothing to do but grab Roxie by the ear.

Dad took the other side. She screamed, but it beat being squashed by the next car.

At the other side, they paused and waited for the others.

Mom and Rockit took off, but timed it poorly. Now they were going to have to sit and let the car go over them. As they looked up at a hot exhaust pipe, the car swerved, narrowly missing them.

Annie flew down to the road, panicked the driver, and he hit the brakes and almost crashed.

Mom and Rockit saw this, ran for their lives, and were now with Dad, Roxie, and Rebel.

"Please tell us, Rebel, that we don't have to that again," begged Roxie.

"Sorry, Buttercup, the next one will be harder."

So back they went to the treetops of the Tree Highway.

This always felt better and the best thing yet was some of the trees were apple trees.

They were all very hungry and the apples were a perfect blessing.

"Mom and Dad, I miss our old home," said Rockit. "I never knew this could be so hard."

"Well, there's no choice, Rockit. We must find a new home and we will."

"Well," said Rebel, "the fabled woods is protected, you'll see."

So off they went, speeding as fast as they could. There were a number of trees they could hide in, as they looked below at the humans playing golf.

Some of the homes had gardens in bloom.

Rebel told them of one he knew where they could steal lettuce and carrots, tomatoes, and corn.

"Problem is," said Rebel, "the humans have a scarecrow to scare the crows, but we can get by that, but they do shoot BB guns at us if they see us."

Dad didn't like stealing but did want some vegetables, the apples caused everyone to want human food. They just didn't want to be targets.

As night approached, they stopped and made camp above the garden.

Tomorrow they would awake early and venture into the garden to get the human food. Then off on the last but hardest day to get to the fabled woods.

CHAPTER 9

CATS

The morning came, once again hazy and cool.

The troupe was so close to a house they could smell the coffee brewing.

"What's that smell?" said Roxie.

"It's bacon, pig's belly, pork!" said Rebel.

"Eww! Humans eat pigs' bellies?" said Roxie.

"Buttercup," said Rebel, "humans will eat anything. That's why they can't run up a tree like us and need cars to get them even 25 feet."

"I'm glad though," said Dad, "imagine if they were on the Tree Highway. Every branch would bend, break, and be gone."

"I'm hungry," said Rockit.

"Yup," said Rebel, "let's raid that garden."

"I've got my eye on about ten things."

"A virtual buffet for a squirrel's delight."

"Let's start with strawberries and polish off with some carrots!"

"Don't you have that backwards, kids?" said Mom.

"Eat your vegetables before you get dessert."

So down to the ground they all went, with Annie hovering above as a scout for any approaching problems.

As they gorged themselves on strawberries, then some carrots, the noise of their little slurps was just enough to get the attention of yet another nemesis to anything small.

"CATS!!!!!!!!!!!" screamed Annie, and sure enough here they came, running as fast as a squirrel.

While the little squirrels wanted strawberries, these two cats wanted red meat—squirrel meat.

"Jeepers!" said Rockit, "Is there ever any peace on this trip?"

Well, one more problem is the cats could climb trees.

Up they went as fast as they could.

"There's only one way we will be safe," said Rebel. Dad agreed and all followed.

"Go to the skinniest limbs at the top. They will not support these fat cats."

And climb they did.

As the cats ran on their way to get them, the little limbs gave out, bent

down, and both cats fell 50 feet to the ground!

"Did you see that?" asked Rockit. "They landed on their feet!"

"Are they related to squirrels?"

"Nope," said Dad, "as far as I am concerned, they are related to the devil, them and snakes, and some say they have nine lives!"

"Cats will kill for fun, not food."

"We're out of here!" and off they scurried heading east into a sunrise in the haze.

The Tree Highway was to stay along the human homes for a few miles.

It was high, pretty, and there was a peace for a while, as most all of the dangerous creatures wanted nothing to do with humans.

CHAPTER 10

INCOMING

"Watch out" screamed Annie, "INCOMING!"

And just as she said this, a golf ball almost hit Mom.

There was a foursome of beginner golfers below and they were driving into the trees, rather than staying on the course.

They all laughed, but would have really been upset being conked on the bottom by a golf ball.

"The fabled forest better be good," said Rockit.

"Oh it is!" said Rebel.

"Why are you so sure and, if so, why do you leave sometimes?" asked Mom.

Rebel responded, "Adventure I guess, Mom. I get lonely when I'm not even alone, so I travel."

"That's fading fast, as I find myself becoming part of the Nutter family."

"That is, if you'll have me," said Rebel.

"Of course, we will," said Mom.

Even Dad was warming up to the sarcastic little smart aleck and Roxie, she was clearly smitten and falling in love.

Rockit was getting the brother he didn't have.

He loved watching the acrobatics of Rebel as he made the journey fun, flipping and flopping, doing summersaults from limb-to-limb.

As they could hear the big road in the distance, the day was going by quickly.

The trees were 100 feet tall and they could see for miles as they danced at the tops.

With each move, the road was getting louder and Roxie was getting very scared.

"Don't worry, Buttercup, I will be by your side all the way," said Rebel.

Horns, screeching tires, the smell of exhaust, and humans were down below—some were walking.

One idea was to travel on the lines of the stoplights.

They decided to try a run between cars again but they had to do it quickly.

"What's that smell?" asked Rockit.

"Hamburgers! A human favorite," said Rebel.

"But you don't want those. I do know behind that drive-in, there's a huge place they throw the uneaten food away."

"French fries and uneaten apple fritters!"

"Those humans serve so much that a lot of it goes uneaten and they throw it out."

"The only problem is we have to be sneaky, because the rats guard it. Not only are they not very nice, they are ugly, and have bad diseases that we don't want. Shoot, even their tails are scary besides their ugly teeth. I don't think they brush."

The road they had to cross was loud and they could see that some of the humans weren't looking where they were going. Some humans would do their best to avoid hitting any squirrels and animals.

"The trouble is," said Rebel, "they are so busy talking on their phones that they don't watch where they are going."

With that, they all gathered in a huddle, sizing up the run.

Annie was so worried. She loved her new family and wished she could fly them across.

"I wish I was the size of Boris," she said.

"I could hold you with my claws gently and fly you over."

But she was small and it was too much of risk. It was time.

31

CHAPTER 11

THE DINER

S o the little troupe, five squirrels and one young woodpecker, gathered at the edge of the road.

Annie flew up to the stop sign wires and scouted.

Rebel decided since he had the most experience at this road, he would lead.

"Good idea," said all, and they awaited his command.

"Annie, what does it look like?" yelled Rebel over the huge noise of the traffic.

"Rebel, after this next car, it looks like they will all stop."

"They're slowing down," replied Annie.

"OK, Nutters, here we go!"

And like desperate but confident runners, off they went.

Looking up in both directions, all they could see was the bottom side of bumpers and smelled the hot rubber of the tires.

"C'mon," said Rebel, "pick it up!"

And pick it up they did. The other side came just as the cars started again, but now the unexpected… cars and humans turning into the diner.

"Quick!" said Rebel, "run to the landscaping at the side of the parking lot."

They all made it, but not before one of the cars screeched to a stop almost crushing Rockit.

"I'm starting to hate this place!" said Rockit.

"It's OK, we are almost at the place where they throw the uneaten food. Let's go."

So they scurried along the fence underneath the plants.

Annie flew above and stopped at the top of a bin—humans call it a dumpster.

The smell of the uneaten food urged them along.

All the excitement made them all hungry.

The back of the dumpster was open, so the humans could throw stuff in easier. In they went.

"My good squirrels, have at it!" said Rebel.

The amount of food being wasted was alarming, but who cared now.

FRENCH FRIES AND APPLE FRITTERS!!

"Maybe we should forget the fabled woods and just stay here."

"It's noisy, but the food just keeps on coming," said Rockit.

And no sooner than he said it, he was grabbed by his tail and a large ugly raspy voice said, "I don't think so, hawk bait!"

"Who do you squirrels think you are?"

They were mortified as this large rat and his gang had them trapped and they looked and sounded like killers. The fright was only surpassed by the fear they would be doomed.

As the large rat moved to do his damage, a voice rang out from under the food.

"LOU, is that you?"

Lou, the rat, turned around and much to all of his surprise, he said, "Rebel, is that you?"

"Yup, Lou, what's your problem with not letting these friends of mine eat some of this stuff?"

"And besides, Lou, you're getting a little broad at the beam and I bet you can't get in your hole!"

"Rebel," said Lou, "you are the only one I'd ever take that from."

"You see, way back, before Rebel's parents were taken by the hawks, they found a little rat and raised him as one of their own."

It was Lou, and he and Rebel, both orphaned the same day, were forever to be brothers.

They went their separate ways, into the woods for Rebel and into trashcans and sewers for Lou.

"He's a rat, that's what they do."

"OK, Rebel, who are these 'friends' of yours?"

"They are the Nutters and the little woodpecker is Annie."

"We all have it in common that a hawk changed our lives so we've united to get to the fabled woods and safety."

"Lou, they are my family now."

"Well," said Lou, "It's all good. I tell you what, Nutters, go to the back—that's where the ice cream and milkshakes are."

"Jeesh, Lou," said Rebel, "ya trying to get them as fat as you?"

"Watch it, little brother, I can still kick your tail."

They all settled down into laughter, french fries, apple fritters, and polished it off with ice cream and a milkshake. Couldn't get any better than that!

33

They decided to spend the night and eat again in the morning.

The Nutters all fell asleep listening to who between Lou and Rebel could tell the biggest lies about all the time they missed being separated.

"Lou, I missed you."

"You were my family, you Rebel— pretty weird, huh?"

"You wanna come with us?" asked Rockit.

"No, thanks," said Lou, "this is a rat's heaven, too much food and no cats anywhere."

"CATS!!!!!!! We hate CATS."

And they fell asleep dreaming. The next day as they parted ways, yet another testy day of danger, then fun, had passed with memories never to fade.

CHAPTER 12

THE FABLED WOODS

As the sun peaked brightly over the eastern edge of the sky, a loud energetic voice said, "Rise and shine, Nutters!!! Today we get to the fabled woods!!" Rebel was beyond ready, as he hurried the Nutters to get on the highway.

"The Tree Highway!"

All were so enthused. They had not had the same place to eat and didn't know for sure where the next meal was coming from, been chased by a savage hawk, ran from cats, dodged a mean owl, and dealt with angry rats. Now it appeared the last day would be jumping, swinging, and leaping from limb-to-limb with the prize in the late afternoon being the fabled woods.

The last miles were in from the roads, high in the tall pines and out of sight from most villains.

"Will we really find our new home Dad?" asked Roxie.

Rebel and Dad answered together, "YUP, Buttercup."

"YES," said Dad.

Dad was almost used to Rebel's manners and that whole Buttercup thing.

Mom could easily see her young daughter was smitten with Rebel.

And why not? Rebel was young, strong, and good-looking.

His manners were that of a young streetwise squirrel whose best

friend was a rat he grew up with.

That came in really handy as Lou, the rat, allowed the Nutters into his private stash of apples fritters and ice cream.

Now off they went, the sun was almost up and they could see nothing but clear skies above.

Roxie tagged along behind Rebel, Dad, and Mom behind, and Rockit was just plain thrilled that a new home was on the way and a new best friend was in his life.

Could it get any better? Well, it was about to.

Rebel was so happy. He was doing barrel roll leaps hanging by his tail, then dropping many feet to spring off the lower limbs, then quickly climbing back to Roxie's side.

It was spectacular!

To Dad, it was showing off—to Mom it was obvious Rebel was going to do anything he can to win the heart of Roxie, and he was.

Annie meanwhile had flown ahead, she was much faster and off she went.

About an hour later, as the little troupe was making progress, she flew back.

She could have stayed in the fabled woods, safe and sound, but instead returned to the side of her new family.

"It's there," she sang. "It's there! I've seen it with my own eyes."

"It's beautiful. There's a stream running fast over beautiful rocks glistening like jewels."

"It meets into a clear blue lake where all the animals come to drink and all seem to get along. Like it's a heaven, where all get along."

"I saw many woodpeckers but I didn't stop to talk with any."

"I just wanted to come back to those who adopted me and share my hopes that I would find my dad and mom. Little did she know that by the next time the sun rose over the fabled woods, she would be reunited with her own parents.

She cried happy tears as she said, "They've never even seen me fly!"

It was near noon and Rebel once again was the tourist guide supreme.

"Look down, there are some wild blackberries!"

This young handsome punk of a squirrel endlessly amazed all, as he seemed to know every last detail of the Tree Highway from good to bad through scary to safe.

"Dad," said Mom, "there is no doubt Rebel has made our lives better in this mission, from homelessness to the soon to be arrival in the fabled woods."

They all ate so many blackberries, they needed to take a nap before carrying on.

It was now noon and Rebel said, "Your next meal will be in the fabled woods, drinking clear spring water from the beautiful stream."

"You will meet the deer, even the raccoons are not bad, and best of all, you're gonna dig the chipmunks like you cannot believe."

"Dad," said Rebel, "we've met all of those animals, what's so new?"

Rebel responded, "Because in the fabled woods everyone gets along, shares and shares alike. It's like the heaven we all wish for."

And with that, they all dozed off for a bit, to be perfectly rested for the last miles.

In a light whisper Roxie could be heard, "I'm so happy, Mom."

Dad went into his snore, Annie just perched high atop a pine tree, and Rockit just dreamed of his new home.

All was good, as the Nutters knew they would soon be once again a family with a home and we all know, there's no place like home, where the heart is.

CHAPTER 13

THE ARRIVAL

Just as every journey starts with one step.

Just as every reality of success starts with a wonderful dream—the travel to find a new safe home, a little woodpecker's parents, and a discovery of family for an orphaned squirrel.

The next leap, next jump, the next swing, has brought to the eyes of the Nutters and friends the distant view of magnificence.

"LOOK!!!!" said Rockit.

"I can't believe my eyes!!" said Mom.

Dad let out a sigh of relief, as he could feel a new security for his family.

Annie flew ahead in tears of joy, as she knew there was the strongest of possibilities she would find her own mom and dad.

And Rebel? He was returning to the fabled woods he left for some reason just days before.

He would come and go many times in his short life, always restless as something was forever missing.

Now he came upon a new day where that emptiness had ceased. Why?

Because he found a family he could embrace, a family that was embracing him, and most of all, he was smitten and falling in love with a love he was always in search of… Roxie.

As the little troupe came to the fabled woods, they all gathered in tears of joy. They had made it.

"Look," said Rockit, "there's a fence around the whole place."

"This would keep many dangers away but not all."

"Why is there a fence?" asked Roxie.

Before Dad could answer, Rebel butted in as usual, "Buttercup, the fabled woods is a protected thing the humans call a 'green belt.'"

"Always to be preserved, safe from buildings, and litter."

Dad didn't mind the interruption for the first time, as he knew Rebel's help proved invaluable.

Rebel made sure they crossed the roads safely, Rebel saved Roxie, and Rebel made sure they ate the best they ever had. Rebel in all of his ill manners was a hero to all.

And, as quickly as they climbed over the fence, several young woodpeckers arrived.

"Annie?" "Is there an Annie in your group?"

"Yes," said Mom, "yes, she's been orphaned her whole life."

"Boris, the mean hawk, tried to kidnap her before she could fly."

"A nice human lady saved her."

"When she was bought back to her tree, all were gone and she's lived in sad loneliness forever."

"We, the Nutters, adopted her as our own, as we started our on search for safety."

"Well," said the oldest of the woodpeckers, "word spread of an unusual family of five squirrels and a woodpecker coming here. We were told of the young Annie and her search for her parents."

"We are here to take her home. I'm her brother and these two are her cousins."

"I'm, Sam, Sam woodpecker, and this is Andy and Polly. Annie is named

39

after the amazing human who saved her."

As the group listened, this dream coming true for Annie, Annie flew back.

"Who are you guys?" asked Annie.

"Annie," said Mom, "these are your family, and they are here to take you home to your mom and dad."

"How on earth did they know I was coming?" asked Annie.

Sam chirped up, "Ya know, Annie, it's the most amazing thing. Some rat named Lou came here. He couldn't clear the fence so he just stood there yelling for any woodpecker to listen. He was a rat. No one likes rats, but he was so persistent we gave his story a chance."

"Rebel, how did Lou beat us here?"

"Most likely, while we were sleeping with our bellies full of blackberries, he pushed ahead. Lou may be fat but he can still run like the wind."

And with that, Annie and her brother and cousins flew off in the dream coming true. Annie was going home.

"Well, where do we go?" asked Rockit.

"Well," said Dad, "I'm sure there's a tree somewhere, hollow in some safe part, and there, if it's available, we will create our new home."

As usual, Rebel said, "Follow me! I've got just the spot." And off they went swinging, leaping, jumping, laughing in a joy and happiness unbridled.

"I know where there's an old Dutch elm, hollow at the top, three entrances, and safe from rain and wind."

Once again, Rebel was saving the day.

"Rebel," said Mom, "why would you ever have left here?"

"Mom," said Rebel, "no matter how many nuts you have, no matter how big your home is, no matter how warm you are on a snowy night, if you live in loneliness, it's all nothing."

"I was heartbroken, lonely, Mom. Then somehow, one day, I needed to find love, family, and a home."

"For the last days, Mom, Dad, Rockit, and Roxie, I've felt all that was missing in my life."

As they proceeded on and arrived at the old Dutch elm, the beauty of the woods was beyond the heaven of any squirrel's hope and dreams.

"Look at that lake! Look at the crystal-clear stream racing over the rocks!! It's just as Rebel said!"

"This place can never change," said Rebel.

"They allow humans to hike for the day on the trails. They can picnic, but they can't start fires or camp."

"Everywhere you will see pictures of large bear warnings that say, 'Only You can prevent forest fires.'"

"There are still hawks, there are still owls, even a snake or two. We can never drop our guard, but it is beautiful and we will never have to cross a road again!" said Rebel.

There was just enough time to gather some grass to place inside the old Dutch elm. They made beds and gathered some leaves to munch on.

"LEAVES!!" said Rockit, "Can't we find some apples?"

As they dozed off, Roxie said, "Rebel, are you sure we can stay here? Will the squirrels this belongs to care?"

"No problemo, Buttercup," said Rebel. "This is my place, my place is now the Nutter's place."

And the most pleasant of feelings came over all, even Dad.

"Tomorrow I will show you the neighborhood. Oh yeah, see that tall soft pine over there? That's your new neighbors—Annie's parents live there."

"We will surprise Annie tomorrow with a good breakfast visit."

CHAPTER 14

THE PROMISED LAND

Tossing, turning, and wiggling, Rockit was so excited he could not sleep. Roxie was no different.

The new home in the old Dutch elm was spacious, warm, and had three views of the fabled woods.

Rebel was in a dead heat of snoring with Dad.

Mom was just plain happy, her entire family was safe and now in a promised land of joy.

No roads and very little humans was the best. Why?

Humans had dogs, and while most dogs would not harm a squirrel, most could not catch one.

Nevertheless, being chased by something ten to twenty times your size is still frightening.

Rebel awoke, yawning and rested. He had only one thing on his mind.

He asked Mom to take Rockit and Roxie outside, jump some limbs, and see all the places they might wish to see first.

Then, he nudged Dad.

"Can I talk with you, Dad?"

"HUH! I'm sleeping."

"This is important," said Rebel.

"OK."

Rebel, voice quivering, paws shaking, started, "Dad, for the first time in my life since I lost my family to Boris, a happiness has returned."

"To be included and become helpful to you and your family has delivered everything I've been wishing for."

"To help you understand roads, help you get to the fabled woods."

"To be able to share my house with you."

"It's been the best thing ever!"

"So," said Dad, "I appreciate it more than I even thought possible!"

"But you are a brash ill-mannered squirrel."

"But after seeing your generosity, your complete dedication to the Nutters, I've changed."

"I once was told by a wise old squirrel, "Never judge a book by its cover.""

"This helped me learn that all the animals in the woods have a story. They might be different colors, different sizes, and even scary, but deep down they are all just like us."

"They just want love and happiness and a family to share it with—even Boris."

"Rebel, what is it that brings you to this conversation?"

Teary-eyed, heart racing, and a bit scared, Rebel responded, "Dad, I want to marry Roxie. I love her, but I want your blessing."

Silently Dad gazed at Rebel, conflicted by the first days, changed by the last days. Dad knew he had to think about it.

"I'll tell you by sundown, I must talk with Mom."

"Fair enough," said Rebel, "Now let's see the woods!!"

Mom, Rockit and Roxie returned and off they went.

"Let's go to the lake first," said Rebel.

"It's always fun and someone new for you to meet."

As they scurried down the old Dutch elm, no one knew what was said while they were gone.

Rebel was nervous, Dad was quiet, but Mom didn't need to be told.

Moms always see ahead and know almost everything about their families, and this was no different.

As they arrived at the lake, the dew on the tall grass where the stream raced in the lake was shining like bright diamonds in the morning sun.

It was absolutely beautiful.

"TOM!!!!!!!!" Well, look who is here, everyone!! It's Tommy turtle."

"He knew my great-great-great-great-great-grandfather. Tommy is over 100 yrs old."

Now Rockit had not been around any turtles and was amazed how Tommy could pull back into his shell.

"Neat!"

"Well," said Tommy, "I know the grass always looks greener on the other side of the fence, but if you had this shell for sure, no one could eat you. However, I find myself envious that you can climb trees, swing from limb-to-limb, and see the best views."

"All I see is the ground, so it all balances out for all. We all have our strengths. The woods made it that way and it's good."

"In differences, we can all learn from each other."

Just then, another morning lake visitor arrived.

"Who are you?" asked Rockit.

"Why I'm Doc duck."

"He's a quack, Rockit."

"SHUT UP, REBEL. I see you have not changed in all your smarty talk."

"Ah, just 'funnin' Doc."

As they all laughed and gazed about, up in the sky there was Annie.

"ANNIE, ANNIE!! Look down. It's us, the Nutters! ME TOO!!" screamed Rebel.

And as quick as a flash, down she came.

"I've so wanted to find all of you today. I found my mom and dad."

"They were beyond happy tears as they thought Boris got me the day I fell."

"It was only a few days ago hope was heightened, that hope was delivered, I might be OK."

"They all can't wait to meet all of you, even Rebel!"

"Even Rebel?"

44

"What kind of stuff is that?" said Rebel.

And with that, they were all off up the soft pine where Annie's family lived. Somehow they all got into the hole. Lou would have never made it.

"Mom, Dad, these are the Nutters. They adopted me as one of their own days ago, as we set out to get to the fabled woods and safety."

"And this is Rebel. We all thought he was a little too harsh and a smarty wise guy, but ya know what—he guided the Nutters through every danger, found them better food, got them across roads they had not crossed, and stopped a rat and his friends from hurting them. Now I hear he will share the old Dutch elm, which has been in his family for many generations."

Mom, Dad, and brother Sam were beyond chirps at the whole story.

They asked if the Nutters ever met the nice human lady who saved Annie.

"No, but we do know Boris snatched Annie by the neck, you bumped him mid-flight, and he dropped Annie from high above. Then you flew off with Boris chasing you out of sight. The humans saw it all from a window and rushed to Annie's side."

"She was terrified—first Boris, then she loses her family, and then a human carefully picks her up, took her inside to safety."

"WOW! What a story."

"Annie never gave up hope this day would come," said her mom.

"We try to raise our kids to never give up, if you have a dream try to make it true, in all things."

"Even love?" asked Rebel.

"Yes, even love, young Rebel."

Dad Nutter just stared… What was he thinking?"

Then it was off just to swing from tree-to-tree, a day of fun scouting out all the new places in the fabled woods.

It was only a day, but a wonderful familiarity grew in the new home, the fabled woods.

Mid-afternoon Rebel, Rockit, and Roxie all took off to play in the highest pines, swaying in wind over 100 feet above the ground. This made the perfect chance for Dad and Mom to talk.

"Mom, do you know what Rebel has asked?"

"Well, it wouldn't surprise me if it's to marry our daughter. Can't you see what he's been doing to win our approval?"

"Yeah, yeah, yeah, but he seems so arrogant."

"Dad, sometimes you confuse confidence with arrogance, cockiness with youth."

"We all were like that at times when we are young. Old squirrels don't know anything!"

"Then, as we age and see the kids realize the older they get, the smarter we were."

"And, Dad, I doubt you will find a love deeper, a more dedicated heart, and a more superb provider for our Roxie ever."

"Well, Mom, you are correct. We couldn't have done this as well without the little punk."

As the kids returned, Dad just looked at Rebel, smiled, winked, and gave him a paws up, Yes.

Rebel took off like a guided missile going from limb-to-limb doing triple summersaults. He was beyond overjoyed.

Tonight after dinner in the clear full moon sky, he would ask Roxie for her hand in marriage.

He dreamed of starting his own family.

Conveniently, the old Dutch elm had two more places to live so she would never be far from her family.

His quest for family was complete.

They all were calm and safe, the fabled woods was real.

The new home was the best the Nutters had ever seen.

It was truly the promised land they had heard about all their lives, and now they were there, safe forever and ever.

hi

hi
Lanai
SKY

CPSIA information can be obtained
at www.ICGtesting.com
Printed in the USA
LVRC01n1615301217
561337LV00001BA/8